TO ALL THE SUPERHEROES BRAVELY FIGHTING THEIR DOUBTS.
AND TO MY FATHER, WHO TAUGHT ME THE WONDERS
OF SPACE AND TIME.
—C.F.

Text © 2022 Tizia-Charlotte Frohwitter

Artwork & Book Design © 2022 Zuzana Svobodová

Title: Novo the Space Robot

Subtitle: How to Shrink the Doubt Monsters (Book 1)

ISBN 978-3-910542-06-8 (Paperback)

ISBN 978-3-910542-07-5 (Hardcover)

ISBN 978-3-910542-08-2 (eBook)

ISBN 978-3-910542-22-8 (Audiobook)

A huge thank-you to the editors, and a special shout-out
to Melissa Richeson, Christie Hainsby, Sally Apokedak,
Nick Sweeney, Luana Horry, and Esther Reisberg.

written by
CHARLY FROH

illustrated by
ZUZANA SVOBODOVÁ

Novo

the SPACE RoBoT

HOW TO SHRINK THE DOUBT MONSTERS

Hello, Earthling!

My name is Novolino, but you can call me Novo—that's what my friends call me. I'm a space robot from the planet Infinita. Yes, it's true—we space-bots do exist!

See? That's me!

Though we live light-years away from Earth, we aren't that different from you earthlings.

We like robo-races, playing fetch with our zogs,
and making lightly buttered veggie batteries to eat.

Sounds like fun, huh? And it is! But we haven't
always lived wonderful, worry-free lives.

One day, everything changed when
unexpected visitors arrived.

They were the DOUBT MONSTERS
from the planet WORRIA!

The creatures drooled an

OOEY-GOOEY

green slime all over the ground . . .

My zapped friends
no longer believed
they could win
robo-races or
make yummy
veggie batteries.

Some bots didn't even think their zogs loved them anymore.

Can you imagine?

It was a nightmare!

And what did the rest of us spacebots do?

Some scattered, scampered, and skittered away in fear.

Some hid
on the sidelines.

And I whispered and whined to my zog.
No-bot-ty knew what to do against the doubt monsters!

The only thing I knew was that I had to find help!

As soon as the doubt monsters turned their backs, I took my chance.

As fast as a mechanical mouse being chased by a space-cat,

I *vroom-vroomed* away on my scooter.

There was no more TICKETY-TICK-TOCK time to lose!

I swooshed through space, zoomed past galaxies,
whooshed into the Milky Way, and headed for
a planet I'd heard amazing stories about:

EARTH!

There, I met little earthlings just like you.

They were

ADVENTUROUS,

CURIOUS
to learn,

EAGER
to try new things,

and they BELIEVED
they could be
whatever
they wanted.

In short:
THEY WERE EARTH-TASTIC!

I was just about to tell them about my emergency when
a cold wave shivered down my robotic spine.

Doubt monsters appeared
everywhere! They must
have followed me to Earth,
trying to take over
the entire universe!
The creatures would start
zap-zap-zapping
everyone with their rays
of doubt in no time!

"THE DOUBT MONSTERS ARE HERE!"

I warned my new earthling friends.

"There will be boredom
instead of adventure,

"RUN AND HIDE!" I shouted.

But the earthlings
didn't move.

"DO NOT KEEP CALM!"

"PANIC!"

"GO!!!!!!"

But the earthlings
still didn't move.
Could they not hear me?
I was sure I'd changed
my voice settings to
Human!

The earthlings decided to do something else.
No scattering in fear.
No scampering and skittering away like
scared squirrels hearing my zog *woof-bloof*.
No hiding, whimpering, or whining.
Now was the time for ACTION!

The earthlings held hands and stared
the doubt monsters down.
And then something super special happened.
A light beamed from the earthlings!
A light from somewhere deep inside them.
A light so strong . . .

. . . it made all the rays of doubt
puff-puff disappear!

"Whoa! How are you doing that?" I asked.

"WE'RE BELIEVING IN OURSELVES!"
an earthling answered.

"Look," another earthling said.
"The doubt monsters
are shrinking!"

And they
shrank . . .

and shrank . . .

. . . and shrank . . .

until they were
the size of cute
little bunnies.

By the wires connecting my screws,
that was the last thing I expected to happen!

One of the earthlings turned to me and said, "Please meet our new friends, the doubt monsters."

I couldn't believe what I was hearing until I saw what was going on with my own laser-eyes.

The small furry fellows really stuck around.
But were they still scary?
No, not at all.

Listen up!

If the earthlings ever started to
doubt they could do something,
they just gave the fluffy doubt
monsters a high-five and
tried anyway.

If the Earthlings didn't like how they
looked one day, they winked at their loyal pals
and realized how special they were.

And if the earthlings were afraid, they **talked their fears away** with their new colorful friends.

Yes, that's right! The earthlings lived happily ever
after with the doubt monsters by their sides.
Now I knew what I had to do!
I waved goodbye to my friends and swooshed back to Infinita.

"Gather around, every-bot-ty," I said to my fellow space robots.
"I have a plan!"

We talked about all the things that made us AMAZING,
and remembered how BOT-TASTIC we were.

And just like that, a light began to shine from deep inside us.
Sure enough, the doubt monsters started to shrink
and shrink and shrink

and shrink

and shrink

and shrink.

Easy-peasy stardust-squeezy!

From that day on, Infinita was
a happy planet once more.

We have the most exciting races,
the yummiest veggie batteries,
the cheekiest zogs, and the fluffiest
doubt monsters.

FINISH

After all, having little doubt monsters around isn't so scary.

Shine brightly, Earthling!

Until next time— Novo, over and out.

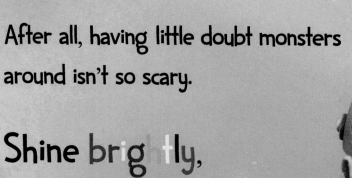

Please help Novo

HELLO, EARTH-TASTIC READER!

I have a favor to ask of you: Could you please help more of us earthlings find out about Novo's adventures by writing a review on Amazon, Goodreads, or any of your other favorite book sites?

That would really mean a lot to Novo!

If you're under thirteen, please ask a grown-up to help you.

Thank you, everyone!

Yours,

Charly

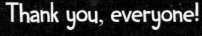

Collect the entire NOVO THE SPACE ROBOT series, and stay tuned for more to come.

Other books from CHARLY FROH

Charly enjoys the magical and the mystical. She loves dreaming about fantasy worlds and typing up their stories. When Charly isn't writing, she's engaging in philanthropic work, adventuring the world, or cooking with her family.

Follow her on Instagram @charlyfroh_author, and visit her website at charlyfroh.com.

Zuzana has been drawing since she could grab crayons. She loves reading books and diving into stories with her two kids. Zuzana's a yogi and a passionate lover of cooking. She always has a cup of good coffee or a piece of great chocolate nearby.

Follow her on Instagram @zuzana_svobodova_illustration, and visit her website at zuzanasvobodova.com.

Made in the USA
Coppell, TX
28 December 2022

90866951R00026